AN~ ~~~~
GREEN KNIGHT

www.realreads.co.uk

Retold by Christine Kidney
Illustrated by Felix Bennett

Published by Real Reads Ltd
Stroud, Gloucestershire, UK
www.realreads.co.uk

ISBN 978-1-906230-86-9

Printed in China by Wai Man Book Binding (China) Ltd
Designed by Lucy Guenot
Typeset by Bookcraft Ltd, Stroud, Gloucestershire

CONTENTS

The Characters   4

Gawain and the   7
Green Knight

Taking things further   55

THE CHARACTERS

Sir Gawain

A loyal and brave young man, Gawain is keen to impress the great King Arthur. His desire to be a good knight puts him in terrible danger. Will he survive?

King Arthur

The legendary King of Camelot is Gawain's uncle. During the great Christmas celebrations he is presented with a strange and horrific challenge. Should he take it on?

The Green Knight

Savage, terrifying, and very green, the Green Knight storms in to interrupt the peace and harmony of the Camelot Christmas festivities. Will he carry out his deadly threat?

The Lord of the Castle

Larger than life and very hospitable, he welcomes the young knight into his home to shelter from the harsh winter as Gawain seeks out the Green Knight. But should he be trusted?

The Lady of the Castle

The most beautiful woman that Gawain has ever seen, she is very kind and friendly to him as he shelters in the castle. Why is she so friendly?

The Old Lady

A curious woman who is always close by the Lady of the Castle. What is it about her that unsettles Gawain? Is there something familiar about her?

GAWAIN AND THE GREEN KNIGHT

Part 1

It was Christmas at Camelot, the court of that king
Whose life is legend, his name so memorable
(Please do me the honour of not nodding off –
It's the tallest of tales in the annals of Arthur
So weird and so wacky you'll say it's a whopper!)
The lords and the ladies all revelled till late
In dancing and drinking, in jousting and japes,
And they feasted a fortnight on fabulous fare.
Then night drew in on New Year's Day
With a banquet prepared of prodigious proportions.
All sat and stared at the star-studded table,
At the canopy covered in sumptuous silk
Where Guinevere graced the great and the good,
King Arthur at her side, Gawain beside his king,
The rest arranged according to rank.
                    She shone,
The brightest belle of the ball.

The beauty is hard to relay
Of that loveliest lady of all –
Her eyes were amazingly gray!

The king was a creature of action and clamour,
He liked nothing less than lazing around.
So instead of tasting the titbits before him
He called for a story, some stirring old saga,
An epic, a pitting of man against peril,
A death-defying tale of derring-do!
Alas, no fable fell from their lips.
The food arrived in full-fettled fanfare
The tables were teaming with taste-tempting treats.
                But look:
It's beyond my powers to describe
The amount they were given that night
And what they chose to imbibe.
(It's really not easy to write.)

The courses were coming in thick and fast
To the tooting of trumpets and the din of the drums,
And just as they ceased their cacophonous cries
A new noise was heard, a nerve-racking roar,
And into the hall hove a hair-raising sight:
A strange colossus, a spine-chilling stranger,
All sinewy strength and bone-crushing bulk;
A gargantuan, jaw-dropping, genuine giant!
(Or half a hulk – it's hard to say.)
In spite of his size, it has to be said
He was a bit of a hunk, a humongous heart-throb,
                    Gigantically gorgeous.
But the gathering gawped and gazed
At this curiosity they'd seen.
Prepare to be amazed:
The man was entirely green!

From top to toe he was decked out in green
With a tailor-made coat tucked into his waist.
His cape was trimmed with tip-top fur,
The purest of pelts, all spotlessly clean.

His manly legs were likewise garbed
In calf-clinging green, and as for his spurs
They sparkled on stirrups that shone with gold.
He dazzled with dozens of different adornments:
The silk of the saddle, its embroidered birds,
The gems and the jewels, all gaudily green.
The overall vision was vividly verdant.
I might have omitted to mention the man
               Sat on
A horse harmoniously hued,
Which strained and pulled at the bit.
But this jade druidic dude
Had complete control of it.

The hair of this hulk hung down to his shoulders,
Bright green and glossy; and his beast of a beard
Seemed to flow like a forest of trees from his face.
And the horse matched its master in mossy green
    glamour –
Its mane was plaited and primped with braids,
Its tail was trimmed with bells and baubles.

Now the knight was noted for his absence of armour,
No helmet, no chain mail, no breast plate, no shield.
All he held in one hand was a sweet sprig of holly,
And a whopping great neck-chopping axe in the other!
He spurred on his steed to enter the hall
And approached the top table with no trace of fear.
'So who's in charge?' he said. 'I'd like
                    A word.'
He cast his eyes across
The gorgeous, knightly gathering
To try and guess the boss,
To spot that famous noble king.

Some seconds slipped by while silence ensued.
A few of the guests tiptoed towards him,
While others were frozen by fear and foreboding.
Then Arthur, with princely politeness and polish
Said, 'Welcome to Camelot, my name is King Arthur.
Please have a seat and a bit of a snack.'
'Not bloomin' likely!' bellowed the big man.
'I'll come straight to the point, if I might be allowed.

Don't flap with fright – I'm not here to fight!
Now, you and your knights are known for your courage,
Your fame is far-flung beyond these great walls,
And because I like to have fun at Christmas
I've taken a notion to set you a dare:
                    Chop off
My head, one blow, right now!
Then give it a year and a day –
I'll return the favour somehow.
So tell me, what do you say?'

No man moved a muscle, nor maiden neither,
But all held their breath at this barbaric business.
'Is this Arthur's house, then?' scoffed the green
        scourge.
'That famous fortress of fearsome fighters,
That glorious garrison of guts and gallantry?
You're having a laugh! You're all lily-livered!
You're a comical crew of knee-knocking cowards!'
Then Arthur, fed up with this vile jeering giant,
Said, 'Are you quite mad, you emerald monster?

Though you howl and holler your lunatic scheme
There's no coward here, no scaredy-cat chicken!
Just give me the axe and I'll do it myself!'
The fiendish freak dismounted his steed;
He stroked his beard and blinked not an eye
While the great king of Camelot took the axe
And waved it unwieldily over his head.
                Then up
Piped Sir Gawain, next to the queen,
'I suppose it's cutting it fine,
But I'm really awfully keen –
Could we make this challenge mine?

If you would see fit, my sovereign lord,
For me to leave the table, right now,
I'd free you forthwith from this fix in a flash –
As long as it doesn't offend the queen –
And stand by your side, or take your place.
And I have to say it's a bit of a cheek,
When the hall is so full of hotshots and heroes,
That you're left clutching that cumbersome
        chopper,

While all gawp and blush on their knightly behinds.
I know I'm not brawny or blindingly bright,
And the loss of my life would lead to no tears.
I'm only a knight because I'm your nephew.
But please don't pursue this preposterous path.
It's really not right that the regal King Arthur
Should stoop to submit to this farcical trick.
Now Fate has seen that I'm first to come forward,
Let me be the fellow to whom it must fall.'
                    The knights
Were quick to approve this idea,
They couldn't be more united!
The king could retreat without fear
Of having his noble name blighted.

The king gave consent for Sir Gawain to rise.
As swift as a dart he dashed from the dais
And knelt before his noble king.
As he heaved the axe into Gawain's hand
The king was grace personified.
He gave Sir Gawain the blessing of God,
And begged him to be both brave and bold.
He favoured his nephew with clever advice:
'Make sure it's a swift and severing strike,
One blow, bish bosh, the ordeal will be over,
And no possible chance he'll ask for payback.'
Without a worry, and wielding the weapon,
Sir Gawain turned to the green intruder.
The giant spoke in his booming bass,
'Now that's all sorted, let's set it straight:
Repeat back to me what you think is in store.'
'I will!' said brave and gutsy Gawain.
'I strike you now and in a year

You'll find
A way to repay the bargain
With any weapon you choose.'
The giant said, 'Right, Sir Gawain!
So, what have you got to lose?'

'By heck!' said the giant, 'You're a gent, Sir G!
I'm happy to face the fate I propose.
With your hand on that axe, make no mistake!
And I don't think you doubt the binding deal
I struck with your sire some moments ago?
But I must have your word, as a man of honour:
Before this gathering of the great and the good,
Do you swear to seek me out, wherever
I may be? And hold it fair
That I refund what I'm about to receive?'
'As God is my maker,' exclaimed Sir Gawain,
'This mystery's starting to make me mad.
How can I promise to stick to this pact?

Just tell me your name and where you abide
And I'll bend over backwards to be there on time,
Cross my heart and hope to die.'
'I'll do you a deal,' declared the green knight.
'When you've hewn off my head I'll happily state
Where I live, what I'm called, where to go –
worry not!
Right, lad!
Stop dawdling and swing that device!
Let's see what you're made of at last.
Come on, get on with the slice!'
Sir Gawain prepared for the task.

The ghoulish green knight took up his position
And bent his head to bare his green flesh.
He flicked his locks right over his head.
Sir Gawain heaved up the axe on high
And swung it down on to green supple skin.
The steel was so sharp it sliced it clean.
The head hit the ground, and hurtled right past
A few of the knights, who kicked it about.

But the monster, whose clothes were
  blotched with blood,
Didn't stumble or stagger or sink to the floor:
He strode across to retrieve his head,
And lugging it by its alarming locks
Mounted his green-maned horse once more.
    He turned
His steed towards the top table,
And to everyone's horror and surprise
They saw something quite incredible:
The severed head opened its eyes.

It began to speak to the silent assembly:
'Sir Gawain has agreed his part in this game;
He knows what is due, there can be
    no doubt.
I'm the Green Chapel Knight, and next
    New Year's Day
He'll come or be called a cowardly chicken!'
He geed up his horse and galloped away,
Still holding that horrible head by the hair.
Sir Gawain still grasped the gore-spattered axe,
In shock at the turn of this dire event.
The knights all laughed, a knee-jerk reaction
Of simple relief that the spook had now scarpered.
King Arthur could see that the boy was bewildered,
And urged him gently to let go the axe.
              'Now look,'
He said, 'don't give it a thought,
It'll do you no good to fret.
Live life, play hard, do sport,
A year is a long time yet.'

Part 2

Who would have guessed when King Arthur got up
And politely requested an epic or poem
That such mind-boggling mayhem would burst
    through the door!
Now it's all well and good when they're guzzling
    from goblets
For folk to forget such frightening affairs,
But the cold light of day will return all their cares.
And so the year passed with pain for our hero,
Who watched every season speed by at a stroke:
The withering winter he witnessed with wonder,
Then shimmering life-giving showers of spring.
The astonishing soul-bursting sizzle of summer
With its flourishing fields, its flowers in bloom,
Turned tamely into an autumn that teemed
Heavy with heart-warming helpings of harvest.
                    The frost
Announced an arctic alarm
For Gawain to get prepared
To face compulsory harm.
He couldn't help feeling scared.

On the first of November the knight said, 'No more;
It's time I tempted my terrible fate.'
The castle was celebrating All Saints Day
And the revels were reaching a riotous racket.
They rarely passed up an excuse for a bash!
They paused, they pitied, they put down their pints;
The noblest of knights now gathered as one –
Ywain, and Eric, and ever so many;
Sir Dod the Dread, the Duke of Clarence,
Lancelot, Lionel, Lucan the Good,
Sir Bors, Sir Bedivere – you get the big picture.
They fussed, they flapped, they feted their friend,
But privately pondered this unpleasant quandary:
Was it worth the waste for such a
             Mad dare?
A party game out of hand
Was risking the life of their friend,
And time was shifting like sand –
He would see it through to the end.

Though Sir Gawain drank in each drop of that day
Next dawn he demanded to dress for his doom.
He asked for his armour: it arrived at the double.
A bright crimson carpet was laid on the floor,
Where great piles of glittering gear were arranged.
He stepped up to start the suiting procedure.
He cut quite a dash in a delightful doublet
And a classic chic cape with a clasp at the neck,
Lined with the loveliest, lightest of pelts.
His feet were set in the shining steel shoes,
And his shins were shod in gorgeous greaves,
And knee-guards so gleaming you could catch your
    reflection
Were laced to his legs with lustrous gold thread.
Then the thigh-guards were fastened with fetching
    thongs.
So the lustrous links of the chain mail descended.
Next arm pieces, elbow guards, gauntlets of steel.
The spurs were last, spiky, stupendous.
He strapped his trusty sword to his side.
Gringolet waited, tack golden and glistening,
As Gawain heaved high his staggering helmet:

Bejewelled and embroidered, a work of art –
Soft silk on the inside, snugly stuffed.
He reached down for his bright red shield
And paused to ponder the pentangle upon it.
A holy sign, he hopes it'll help.
So this was it!
He made a mental checklist:
Armour, horse, and nerve.
They fussed and said he'd be missed.
Then he left for the cause he must serve.

Sir Gawain set out with grim resolve,
Scouring the north in search of a sign,
Never stopping for fun or a friendly feast,
Lonely, as if God no longer loved him.
Each person he passed, he posed the same question:
'Do you know where to find the green knight?'
He got some odd looks from perplexed passers-by.
He scrambled up mountainsides, forded fast
     streams,
Fighting each foe with phenomenal pluck.

You wouldn't believe the abominable beasts –
I can only manage to recount a mere tenth.
He duelled with dragons, he warred with wolves,
And sometimes with wodwos (vile woodland weirdos).
He battled with bulls, and bears, and boars.
                    Oh, and ogres.
But worse than the fear and fighting
Was the sheeting, freezing rain.
Those shards of ice were biting,
And caused him incredible pain.

At night he slept rough under great craggy rocks
Where daggers of ice dangled over his head.
Each day a new trek across treacherous terrain,
The countryside stripped quite bare and barren
As winter waged its woeful war.
Gringolet grittily made it through mud
And marsh and mire with remarkable mettle.
Then on Christmas Eve Gawain prayed to Christ
For some sign, some succour, some sheltering
        sanctuary.

The very next second he halted his horse:
As if by magic, a magnificent moat,
And a castle – incredibly, colossally great –
Rose out of the shimmering shallows below.
Its unreal enormity awed Gawain:
He'd never seen such spires, such stonework, such strength
Built for battle but embellished for beauty.

He stopped
And wondered if there was a chance
He might be invited inside
To shelter, to feast, to dance
For the rest of this cold Christmastide.

A porter appeared and bade him approach.
The drawbridge descended and a large delegation
Drove out in a dizzying whirlwind of welcome.
Horse stabled, he staggered with help to the hall
(He ached in the armour he'd worn for ages)
Where a fire blazed with fearsome force.
Then the lord of the castle came out of his chamber,
Larger than life, with a bright red beard,
And embraced Sir Gawain as his cherished guest.
Our knight nearly reeled with grateful relief.
He was led to a chamber of delicate charm,
Where at last he stripped off the burdensome steel,
And was clothed in the softest, luxurious silks.
The feast that followed was fabulously filling
But no food could compare with the wife of the lord,

Whose beauty was greater than Queen Guinevere's.
Sir Gawain couldn't believe his eyes.
And by her side was an ancient dame
Who unsettled Sir Gawain in some mysterious way.
Christmas Day came and the carousing commenced;
They danced and feasted for two long days.
Gawain would gladly have stayed there for good,
But two days after Christmas he confessed his fate
And told the great lord he must leave by next light.
It all poured out, his pitiful plight
Of how he must track down the dreaded green ghoul.
The lord just laughed and said 'Leave it to me;
I guarantee you'll get there on time.
And while I'm out hunting make this place
     your home.'
As Gawain gratefully grasped his great hand.
The lord laughed again and loudly declared:
               'I know!
To give it an extra lift
Let's have a little game:
What I win I'll make you a gift,
And you'll do exactly the same.'

Part 3

In the early hours the servants were up
As the hunters hoisted themselves from their beds.
They took mass, munched breakfast, and made
    themselves ready.
These guests called their grooms and gave them orders
To sprint to the stables and tack all the horses.
They sprang to their saddles with superiority,
Their leaps expressing the best of society.
The hounds were unleashed from their
    crowded kennels
And howled and hurtled headlong for a scent.
The burst of the bugle boomeranged round
Mixed in with the sound of snarling and snapping,
And beaters barged through the braying forest
Sending waves of fear through the overwrought
    wildlife.
A herd of terrified deer was trapped
As arrows rained down on their shivering flanks.
Some escaped, but were traced to the silvery stream
And savaged by dogs or set on by men.

A hollering hellish noise was heard,
A mixture of slaughter and brutish delight.
    And so
The day was spent in such sport
The riding, the killing – such fun!
But the pleasure was cut short
By the sight of the setting sun.

But let's reel back to earlier that day
And return to the castle, where our Christian knight
Was having a long and well-deserved lie-in.
At sun-up he snoozed and stayed fast asleep
Until the opening sigh of the door
Whispered the arrival of a morning visitor.
Around the bed were beautiful hangings
Hiding the knight from the unknown intruder.
Gawain dared to peep from a slit in a drape,
And much to his amazement saw
The dazzling dame, tiptoeing towards him.
He dived back under his capacious covers,
And lay there stone still as if in sleep.
He quietly panicked as it wasn't quite proper,
And hoped she'd heave-ho if he gave her the hint.
        No luck!
She sat on the edge of his bed
While he lay there as still as a statue,
But soon he gave up playing dead
As she said, 'Good morning to you.'

He signed the cross as if in shock,
Nervous, not knowing the next move.
She laughed with a light and lilting chuckle.
Now the thing about knights is they fear offending,
So although Gawain was trapped and embarrassed
He had to politely pretend and prattle
With the choicest of courtly chit-chat and customs.
A knight must vow love but decline to claim it –
A complicated, confusing chivalrous code.
So he flattered, faint-heartedly, flustered and
    flummoxed
As compliments cascaded from her captivating
    mouth.
He must compliment back, but bear in mind
The lord, his host, whose lady lingered.
                    At last
She moved as if to go
But turned and surprised him with this:
'A gift, my gallant hero,'
And bent down to give him a kiss.

34

While these words were exchanged in such
    wistful warmth,
Back in the woods the butchery began.
The gruesome gralloching gathered apace,
The skillful carving of kill into meat.
They scooped out the stomachs and stripped back
    the skin,
Chopping and cleaving the choicest cuts.
The dogs devoured the discarded bits,
And the workers were paid for their participation.
The rest hauled up the hewn herd on huge spikes
And veered towards home with their valuable
    venison.
The fires raged in the hall's great hearth
As the hunters presented their fleshy prizes.
'What do you think?' thundered the lord
To Gawain, who gaped at the gargantuan horde.
'I don't remember seeing more meat –
It's a pretty prodigious pile,' he replied.
'It's all yours,' whooped the lord with a whopping
    great laugh,
'As per our agreement. Perhaps you've a present?'

'Oh yes!'
Gawain lunged at the lord with a kiss,
Who exclaimed, 'What's this tomfoolery?
'How on earth did you come by this?'
'That,' said Gawain, 'stays a mystery.'

They feasted for hours as friends that night,
But at crack of dawn the hunt recommenced.
The hollering hounds, the hurtling steeds,
In plunging pursuit of some suitable prey.
They ranged across acres of savage terrain,
Then the dogs sniffed out an exciting scent
And the hunters gathered hard on their heels.
A boar broke free from brackenish cover.
A staggering swine, a porcine warrior,
Charging about in search of escape.

The bugle was blown for back-up, because
The arrows were bouncing off the boar's back.
The tormented creature turned on his attackers
And charged toward them with an ear-splitting squeal,
And injured a group with a lunging gouge.

He fled.
Some hunters chose to retire,
But the lord continued to chase
This creature through thicket and mire.
To turn back would mean losing face.

Sir Gawain slumbered in blissful sleep
As master and men proved their real might.
He dreamt with delicious, oblivious abandon
While the hog was hunted to ground by hounds.
He woke to the whispering voice of a woman –
She was sitting beside him once more on the bed
And before he could counter she gave him a kiss.

They lounged and lolled and talked of *lurve*
For hours, it seemed – the subject is endless.
She asked, how come a courtly knight
Who must be versed in the ways of love
Refused to teach his towering knowledge?
Gawain was gripped by guilt and confusion –
It was a delicate dilemma the dame put him in.
Avoid and offend this flattering female,
Or outrage his host with a dangerous gesture?
But before he could come to a happy conclusion
The lady gave him another kiss.
                    He felt
He'd done no very great wrong,
And relaxed as he spent the day
In refined conversation and song –
It was the courtly way.

The boar battled on with brutish bravery
No coward, he coursed and crashed through woods,
All fixed to fight with his human foe.
Some scattered in serious fear of the swine.

The hog grew tired and started to hobble,
And found a spot by the side of the stream.
Most of the men dared not approach,
But the master dismounted with
     consummate ease
And stomped towards that petulant pig.
The hairs on the back of the hog grew high,
And he lunged at the lord with feral blood-lust.
They fought for their lives in the babbling brook
As those who looked on were clueless.
         Who would win?
But the master soon plunged his great sword
Into the neck of the hog, like a lance.
The others began to applaud –
The swine never stood a chance!

The boar was beaten but continued to breathe,
So the dogs dived in and dragged it away.
They quickly killed it, then continued to chew,
But before the hounds could hack it to bits
The head of the hunt commanded them stop.

One of the band, a bushcraft butcher,
Started to carve up the slaughtered creature:
The head was hacked off as a hunting trophy,
And the carcass was slit and sliced with skill.
The intestines were toasted as treats for the dogs.
They put the pig on a very long pole,
And wended off home with their hard-won prize.
Again Gawain was granted the gift
Of this big pile of pork, what a perfect present.
                    In return
He gave his host two kisses,
Who raised a questioning brow,
But Gawain dismissed it,
Saying, 'Please don't ask me how.'

As soon as dawn broke the hounds were unbound
And charged to the hoot of the hunting horn.
Dashing about in search of a scent,
They fixed on the powerful whiff of a fox.
He ducked and dived, determined to flee
The stupid dogs, those slobbering dumbos.

All day the fox frustrated his foes.

Gawain meanwhile enjoyed his last lie-in

As tomorrow he must tramp towards his doom.

As he dreamt and dozed, the dame tiptoed
Back to his bedroom to bombard him
    with flattery.
She asked for some token, a souvenir to treasure,
But so far from home he had nothing to offer.
Around her waist she wore a girdle,
Green silk, embroidered with golden thread.
She took it off and gave it to Gawain.

He said he couldn't possibly accept
But she wore him down again, and when
She whispered that it had special powers
He found it surprisingly hard to resist –
For whoever wore this beautiful belt
Would be protected from physical injury.
    Yes, whoever
Wore this beautiful belt
Would be protected from harm,
Whatever blow was dealt –
It had a magic charm.

With courtly grace she gave him three kisses,
Leaving Gawain in a clash with his conscience –
Give up the girdle, as agreed in the game,
Or hide it, hang on to it, however dishonest,
For what other hope did our hero have?
The fox was finally run to ground
Despite its dog-defying tricks.
The valiant vulpine was finally vanquished.

The master sliced the finishing stroke
And skinned the creature's pitiful pelt.
Gawain was first to exchange his gift –
Hurling himself at his host with three smackers
                    'By heck!'
Said the lord, 'A triple gift
Outshines this fox's skin!'
Trying not to fidget and shift,
Gawain cloaked his face in a grin.

Part 4

New Year's Day dawned, the dark disappeared,
And the cold light of day commanded Gawain.
The moment had come to move on, man up.
He loaded on the elaborate armour,
Resplendent, refulgent, with the rust
        now removed.
He dressed himself with a servant's assistance.
He grabbed the green and gold girdle
And wrapped it twice round his steel-clad waist.

Reunited with his rested horse he rode
Over the drawbridge, desperately sad,
For here he found a fine and fierce friendship.
The servant set him on the right road.
Through freezing fog they felt their way
In search of the chilling and gruesome
    green chapel,
And then without warning the servant
    stopped dead.
'You have reached your destination,' he said.
'I'm not remaining to meet that madman,
A bloodthirsty brute who butchers humans.
I'm off, and if you'd follow my advice –
        Run now!
I promise I won't tell a soul.'
Gawain said, 'Do you suggest
I'm a coward with no self-control?
I will stay, and fulfil my quest!'

Great words aside, Gawain was worried,
But persevered despite his distress.

He hacked his horse heroically down
The side of a steep and slippery slope.
His legs gripped Gringolet as they
 gingerly descended
To a grim and godforsaken gully.
Each side of the valley stretched up to the sky
Where craggy rocks seemed to scrape the clouds.
But a chapel? Gawain could find no such thing –
Just a funny-looking knoll up ahead
Beside a stream that surged with spume
From the force of the water that flowed there.
He dismounted his horse and went to explore:
A peculiar lump growing out of the ground.
He counted three holes – could they be entrances?
A chill swept up Sir Gawain's spine
He sensed the cave was incredibly creepy,
The kind of hole that hulk would hang out in.
   Ssswhack! What's that?
A hideous noise rent the air,
Our hero felt disheartened.
Ssswhack! He began to despair:
The sound of an axe being sharpened!

'Who's there?' called Gawain, with more guts
    than he felt,
'Show yourself now! I must insist!'
'Hold your horses!' hollered a voice.
'I can't see the reason you're in such a rush.'
Shwaannng! The axe was swiped against stone.
Then out of the cave the freak came flying,
Hurling the axe high over his head
(Gawain discerned a Danish model)
A bloodcurdling brute of a barbarous blade!

The gruesome giant was as green as ever
And vaulted the stream in one vast stride,
Carrying the axe like the lightest of sticks.
'Well,' he said when he reached Gawain,
'You've kept your promise, my punctual prince.
Are you man enough to meet the same fate
As I submitted to, twelve months ago?'
                    'I'm here,
Aren't I?' said a vexed Gawain.
'What more can you possibly want?
Now strike – just once, not again!'
How he tried to sound nonchalant!

The axe swung high and as it came down
Gawain cowered the teensiest bit.
'What have we here?' jeered the green knight
As he lowered the lethally worrying weapon.
'Sir Gawain – a gutless and grovelling
      goofball?'
'Look, I just flinched a fraction, all right?
Get on with it now, stop messing around!'

He flexed his head, but instead of a felling
The axe fell away as it fluttered through air.
'For goodness' sake!' growled Sir Gawain,
'Get on with it, will you, you merciless weirdo?'
It's the teasing and torment he could not abide –
He'd rather his head was hacked off in a hurry.
'If you insist,' sneered the green savage.
The axe came down in a slicing swoop,
And nicked our knight on the side of the neck.
He saw a splash of blood hit the snow,
And leapt like lightning away from the spot,
Ready to fight his fearsome foe.
'That's it! One strike! That's all you get!
I've stuck to my side of this stupid bargain!'

'Hang on!'
Said the green knight with a smile.
'The game is over, don't fret.
You've proved you're a knight without guile;
Let's call an end to this bet.'

Gawain was reeling at the green man's response
And couldn't believe what he went on to hear:
'When my wife bestowed her sweet, tempting kisses
I could hardly believe how you handed them over.
Despite her teasing you were defiantly decent –
Otherwise, honestly, I'd have hewn off your head.
The slice in your skin is for the gift you kept:
My own silk girdle, sewn by my wife.'
Gawain was dismayed at his show of weakness.
He tore off the girdle and ranted a while
About cowardly concern for staying alive,
And how he'd broken the courtly code.
'Look, why not keep it?' countered the ghoul,
'And let it remind you you're only human.'

He then explained to a shocked Gawain
That the whole episode was a priceless prank,
A jolly good joke to play on the king.
The elderly lady who lives with his wife
Was Morgan le Fay, once a student of Merlin's
And the sister – and enemy – of their sire,
    King Arthur.
(And so, amazingly, our hero's aunt!)
        She charmed
This man into miraculous green
And showered some spells for protection.
Now, to show his deepest esteem,
He invited Gawain back with affection.

Sir Gawain said, 'God thank you, kind sir,
But I really must return to my home.
Yet before I go, may I beg your name?'
'It's Sir Bertilak de Hautdessert!'
Said his former foe. They bade farewell
And exchanged some charitable Christian wishes.

Despite this decorous and dashing departure
Sir Gawain made his mortified way
Back to Camelot, his conscience in turmoil.
He was greeted with stunned and grateful
    amazement
(They weren't expecting him back in one piece).
An embarrassing blush spread across his face
As he explained that he was no conquering hero.
He recounted the whole story to an astounded
    audience.
He lamented his love of his own human flesh,
And chided himself for his craven cowardice.
They let him rant on with warm-hearted
    patience,
They paused, they pondered, then Arthur
    piped up:
'Let's all agree to wear a green girdle!'
And so they eased Sir Gawain's shame
By sharing the sign of his self reproach.
And instead it became an illustrious badge
Of those long-lost legendary lords of Camelot.

And so
I hope you won't think badly
As my tale arrives at its end
And I take my leave of you sadly.
May God go with you. Amen.

TAKING THINGS FURTHER

The real read

This *Real Reads* version of *Sir Gawain and the Green Knight* is a retelling of an original poem written in the late 1300s. No one knows who the author of this poem was and he or she is just referred to as 'the *Gawain* poet'. There is only one single copy in the British Library in London, a manuscript so small that it would fit in the palm of your hand. It was lost for a long time, then rediscovered in the Victorian period. It makes you wonder how many other great manuscripts have been lost and never rediscovered.

The original poem is written in Middle English, which is very hard for most readers to understand. Even some of the letters look different. Middle English is a mixture of Old English, influenced by Saxon, French, and each region's own particular dialect. When *Gawain* was written, many areas of Britain had their own very distinct ways of talking and writing.

You may have noticed that the poem is 'alliterative', with the same sounds repeating at the beginning of nearby words or on the stress of a word – for example

He called for a story, some stirring old saga
An epic, a pitting of man against peril.

The poem doesn't rhyme all the time, but the stresses or beats often fall on the same letter. This is very typical of the poetry from the area we believe the *Gawain* poet to be from, Cheshire in the north-west of England. We have retained this stress pattern in our version, as it emphasises the pace and humour of the original.

Another important feature of *Gawain* is the 'bob and wheel' at the end of each verse – the 'bob' is a very short line, sometimes of only two syllables, followed by the 'wheel', usually four longer lines, which rhyme in alternate pairs.

If you want to see what *Gawain* looks like in the original Middle English, there is an edition edited by Norman Davis and J.R.R. Tolkien (the author of *Lord of the Rings*). The best complete modern version is by the poet Simon Armitage which, like the *Real Reads* version, keeps to the original verse form.

Filling in the spaces

The poem is not very long, so we haven't had to cut out any really important events in the poem. We have however had to leave out some of its wonderful detail.

At the beginning of the original poem there is a statement from the poet placing the poem in its historical context, going back in time to the founding of Rome. We have left this out, as it is not an essential part of the story. An introduction like this was common in medieval epic poems, designed to demonstrate to listeners that this was a really important and interesting poem.

The detail we have left out gives you an even fuller picture of what life was like in medieval England, both at court and in the countryside. The details about the court provide wonderful descriptions of the sumptuous food and the delicate and luxurious clothes. There are long passages describing the armour Gawain puts on, which can almost make you feel as if you are wearing the heavy steel armour yourself.

The poem also demonstrates the author's detailed knowledge of the countryside, and what it was like when travelling was much harder than it is now. There is a long passage when you can feel Gawain's pain as the rain lashes him like sharp knives of ice as he rides on his wintry search for the Green Chapel.

Back in time

The legend of Arthur became very popular in the medieval period, and if you watch films and look at pictures depicting Arthur and his court you will almost always see them dressed in medieval costume. In fact, if Arthur actually existed at all he was probably a warrior fighting the Saxons at the end of the Roman occupation of Britain in the sixth century.

The most famous writer at the time of the *Gawain* poet was Geoffrey Chaucer, who wrote *The Canterbury Tales*. Not only is this a brilliantly funny poem depicting medieval life in all its colour, it is very important because it is written in English.

French had been spoken at court since the Norman invasion in 1066. Chaucer and the *Gawain* poet were writing over two hundred years later, during the reign of Richard II. At this period language of literature was changing from French to English, though the official language used at court did not change until Henry V's reign, round about the time he set off to fight the French at Agincourt in 1415. Many scholars think that one of the reasons for King Arthur becoming so popular at this time is that people wanted a real 'English' hero.

The most popular writer of medieval romance was a French poet called Chrétien de Troyes, who enhanced the Arthur myth and introduced Sir Lancelot and the Holy Grail. These do not feature in *Gawain*, but many of those who read *Gawain* would also have been familiar with Chrétien de Troyes.

The most famous book about Arthur appeared nearly a hundred years after *Gawain*, in 1485 – *Le Morte d'Arthur* by Thomas Malory. This is probably the most famous medieval book about King Arthur and his knights.

Finding out more

We recommend the following books, websites and films to gain a greater understanding of the world of Gawain.

Books

- Simon Armitage, *Sir Gawain and the Green Knight*, Faber, 2007.

- T.H. White, *The Once and Future King*, Harper Collins, new edition 2015.

- Philip Reeve, *Here Lies Arthur*, Marion Lloyd Books, 2011.

- Michael Morpurgo, *Arthur, High King of Britain*, Egmont, 2008.

- Michael Morpurgo, *Sir Gawain and the Green Knight*, Walker Books, 2015.

- Kevin Crossley-Holland, *The Seeing Stone*, Orion, 2001.

- Terry Deary, *The Measly Middle Ages*, Scholastic, 2007.

Websites

- www.bbc.co.uk/history/ancient/anglo_saxons/arthur_01.shtml
A comprehensive BBC website, with a section written by Michael Wood, one of the most interesting historians specialising in this period.

Films and TV

- *The Sword in the Stone*, animated film, directed by Wolfgang Reitherman, 1963.

- *In Search of the Dark Ages*, Michael Wood series, BBC, re-released 2015.

- *A Knight's Tale*, directed by Brian Helgeland, 2002.

- *Merlin*, BBC series 1 to 5, released 2013.

Food for thought

Here are a few things to think about if you are reading *Sir Gawain and the Green Knight* alone, or ideas for discussion if you are reading it with friends.

Starting points

● What impression do you have of King Arthur? Do you think the poem portrays him as the great king of legend?

● What do you think about the knights who don't accept Arthur's challenge?

● Do you feel sorry for Sir Gawain? Is too much being asked of him? Would you have confessed to having the green girdle?

● Do you think this is a poem about a great legendary knight, or about a human being in an impossible position? Where do you think the poet's sympathies lie?

● Look at the contrast between the hunting scenes and Sir Gawain snoozing away in his luxurious chamber. Although it is Gawain who goes out looking for the Green Knight, who do you think is actually being hunted?

● Who do you think wins in this Christmas game? Who is it that has the last laugh?

Themes

What do you think the *Gawain* poet is saying about the following:

- honesty
- bravery in the face of an inevitable fate
- how to live up to an ideal
- loyalty
- nature versus the comforts of the court

Style

Can you find passages in the poem containing the following:

- pathetic fallacy, where the description, perhaps of the landscape or the weather, seems to reflect the mood of the main character
- irony, where the poet might be laughing at the characters, maybe by making a very serious point offset by a funny comment
- symbolism, such as the pentangle on Gawain's sword being a protective sign

- alliteration, with the same sounds repeating at the beginning of nearby words or on the stress of the word

- four main stresses or 'beats' in each of the longer lines – a *te-tum te-tum te-tum te-tum* rhythm – the sound pattern that much of the original *Gawain* was written in

- 'bob and wheel', a very short line of two syllables, followed by four longer lines which rhyme in alternate pairs

Try your hand at writing some lines with the four-main-beat *te-tum te-tum te-tum te-tum* rhythm. See if you can also include some alliteration – you may well find it easier than you think.

When you have done that, you can try your hand at a 'bob and wheel' too. Before long you'll have the beginnings of your own medieval poem.

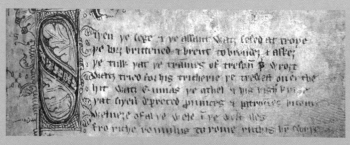

Part of the *Gawain* manuscript in the British Library